Enid Blyton's

Night-time
TALES

Text copyright is the property of Enid Blyton Limited
(a Chorion company). All rights reserved.

ISBN 978-1-84135-405-7

Text copyright © Enid Blyton Limited
Enid Blyton's signature is a trademark of Enid Blyton Limited

First published 2000 by Award Publications Limited
This edition first published 2005
Third impression 2007

Published by Award Publications Limited,
The Old Riding School, The Welbeck Estate,
Worksop, Nottinghamshire, S80 3LR

www.awardpublications.co.uk

Printed in China

Enid Blyton's

Night-time
TALES

AWARD PUBLICATIONS LIMITED

The Stories

1
The Toys' New Palace

Illustrated by Pamela Venus

Jack and Tilly had built a palace with their bricks. It was a very good one – very tall and grand, with windows and a door and lots of towers and turrets. The children were pleased with it.

"It's a pity nobody ever lives in the houses and palaces we build," said Tilly. "They are just wasted, really. We build them, and then we knock them down."

"I wish we didn't have to knock *this* palace down," said Jack, looking at it proudly. "It really is one of the best we've ever made, don't you think? Look, Mummy! Don't you think our palace is good?"

"Splendid!" said Mummy. "But now it's time for bed so you must put your bricks away."

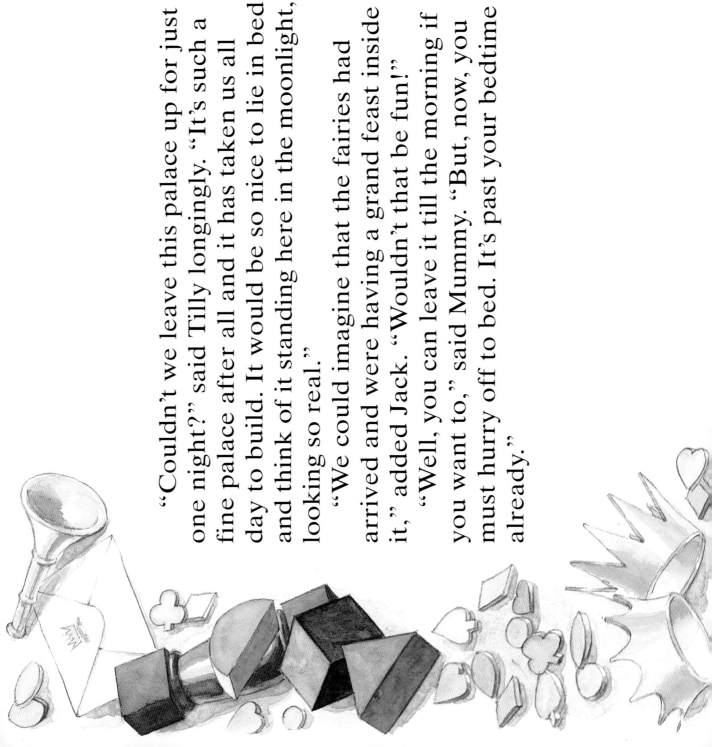

"Couldn't we leave this palace up for just one night?" said Tilly longingly. "It's such a fine palace after all and it has taken us all day to build. It would be so nice to lie in bed and think of it standing here in the moonlight, looking so real."

"We could imagine that the fairies had arrived and were having a grand feast inside it," added Jack. "Wouldn't that be fun!"

"Well, you can leave it till the morning if you want to," said Mummy. "But, now, you must hurry off to bed. It's past your bedtime already."

Little did the children realise that, as soon as they had left the room, their toys all started to come to life. The big teddy bear let all the toys out of the toy cupboard. The dolls woke up inside the doll's house. All the animals on the toy farm came awake and the clockwork train started running about all over the floor.

It happened every night and this night the toys were pleased to find that the children had left them a splendid palace to play in. They thought it was a very fine present indeed!

When the children were safely in bed, and the nursery was in darkness except for the big silver moon shining through the window, the big teddy bear ran right across the nursery floor and looked through the doorway of the fine wooden palace.

"I say! It's the best thing that ever was!" he called. "Come on toys! Look what the children have built for us! See this window – and that one – and look at the turrets and spires at the top. My, haven't they built it well!"

"It's splendid," said one of the dolls' house dolls. "Can we go inside?"